A Small Life

Suki

CinnamonPress

INDEPENDENT INNOVATIVE INTERNATIONAL

WITHDRAWN

D0494152

Published by Cinnamon Press
Meirion House
Glan yr afon
Tanygrisiau
Blaenau Ffestiniog
Gwynedd LL41 3SU
www.cinnamonpress.com

The right of Susan Vickerman to be identified as author and artist of this work has been asserted by her in accordance with the Copyright, Designs and Patent Act, 1988. © 2012 ISBN 978-1-907090-75-2
British Library Cataloguing in Publication Data. A CIP record for this book can be obtained from the British Library

All rights reserved. No part of this publication may be reproduced, stored in a retrieval system, or transmitted in any form or by any means, electronic, mechanical, photocopying, recording or otherwise without the prior written permission of the publishers. This book may not be lent, hired out, resold or otherwise disposed of by way of trade in any form of binding or cover other than that in which it is published, without the prior consent of the publishers.

Designed and typeset in Palatino by Cinnamon Press
Cover image: © Judi Rich Cover design by Jan Fortune
Printed in Great Britain by the MPG Books Group, Bodmin and King's Lynn
Cinnamon Press is represented in the UK by Inpress Ltd and in Wales by the Welsh Books Council

A Small Life is a work of fiction in which no character represents any living person. For this writer, as for many writers, experiences and encounters serve as useful triggers for the development of fictional scenarios. The intimate internal thoughts of Suki do not equate with the internal life of the author. For a sample of what Sue Vickerman really thinks about whilst in pose as a life model (like Suki, it's her day job), go to the famous Redbrick Mill blogging site www.tornwood.typepad.com and read the September 2011 archive entitled 'Two Day Life Drawing 17-18 September'.

The publisher acknowledges support from Arts Council England Grants for the Arts

743·4 SOK

19.3.13

741·092

A 8013 IL

LOTTERY FUNDED

Acknowledgements

Thank you Muse-in-Chief Alison Marshall for your spot-on advice, and Phil Jones, Becca Clare and Jean Harrison for encouragement about my first draft. Thank you Sam Firth my wizzo computer butler and Jonathan Glover for advice on images, and life-model Caroline Kelly for allowing use of drawings of us both. For the cover portrait, thank you Judi Rich, also Dave Thomas (Grassington Group) for much e-discussion and many mock-ups, and Keith Lowe (The Saturday People, Leeds) for messing about with images for me. Thanks Michael Kilyon for the QR codes and composer Stuart Field (Alternative Choices Ltd, Birmingham) for use of your recording studio.

For the bookings that have paid my bills and given me the inspiration and images for this book, I am grateful to many artists, co-ordinators and tutors. Thank you Carine Brosse (Grassington Group), Ellie Halls Schiadas at Leeds Gallery, Jane Fielder at Bingley Gallery (Cullingworth Group), Roma Crossland and Helen Peyton of Granary Arts at Skipton Castle, Justyn Tandy and Laura Brennand of Craven College in Skipton, Susan Forster-Ross of Ilkley, Sam Dalby in Settle, Lindsey Holden and Nicola May of Bradford Drawing Group, Tony Noble at Redbrick Mill, and John Bolland of The Saturday People, Leeds.

Hear Suki's voice

Suki has audio-recorded the five poems appearing in this book. Just run the scanner of your Smartphone or Blackberry over the QR code (square bar code) printed next to the poem and listen.

Visit www.sukithelifemodel.co.uk

Please visit my site and share your thoughts on art, poetry, life, death, loneliness, the search for a raison d'être, and the quest for love. Upload your drawings if you like. You will also find 'Life-drawing opportunities in Yorkshire', 'Book me' (for readings/modelling), my gallery, and more...

Also by Suki: KUNST (Indigo Dreams Publishing, 2012)

A poetry pamphlet themed on the artist-model relationship. Includes monochrome images by sixteen artists and QR codes for audio-poems.

Contents

Spring

Summer

The Beginning

One day I was drinking a latte in Paolo and Nathan's lovely manor on the village green when their friend Gordon dropped by. Gordon found my face striking and, later, recommended me to his friend Jeremy, an artist who lives in a tumbledown cottage near the river.

I agreed to sit for a portrait as a volunteer.

Suki, the Artist's Model.

Jeremy spent thirty-six hours over the summer painting my head and shoulders. During these sessions it emerged that he had trouble finding life-models.

It is paid work and I am a penniless writer. For this surface reason, I have offered myself.

Autumn

First time 'kit off'

This is all very formal. I am keeping to his emailed instructions. I change in another room. Jeremy has already arranged the lighting, the stool, the drapery. He has an exact precise pose in his head. Verbally he sets me up in it – I am not a bowl of fruit he can poke about with. He puts the Vivaldi on, I pull my frock off.

It's not sexy at all.

As per the many hours we have already spent together in this room, we remain silent. I mean completely wordless. Hence, as I did for the portrait, I lose myself in my head. For once, a tear does not eventually, slowly, climb out and roll down   (I have had to pass these off as a reaction to turps).

There's the usual piece of cake at half time (how come he's so slim and fit?). I make conversation about my new exercise regime now that my novel's with an agent. I tell him I've got out of shape through sitting at my desk writing for the last four years. I boast that this agent's really up there; she's got an Orange Prize winner on her list and I've just had to post her my complete manuscript as she 'loved' the first three chapters.

Blah blah blah. He is picking up his palette with a distracted look. I feel a fool.

Size 14, if you don't mind

That's a size 16 bottom you've drawn! I don't say.

Jeremy perceives me as fat. So he definitely doesn't find me attractive.

At least I'm being paid for some of the important staring into space I do. I tell Jeremy I want more of this work. He says he'll ask a friend.

At break time I chat about what I'm reading. Jeremy chats a bit about Art and Music (he isn't into literature). As always, there's no eye contact.

I like this lonely walk home in the damp dark. Kicking through this lovely decay. Until unexpectedly my womb starts tipping itself out. A deluge. I have to scurry.

What would I have done?

I hurry into my empty cottage (empty of my manuscript). I sit on the toilet for ages. I am at a loose end, so I work on a poem.

Sitter

She would make him sit just so: stripped bare,
muscular, circumcised, white skinned, elegant, shivery;
would rip masking tape from a roll to mark round his toes
on the carpet, round his hand on the chair.

This would stop him from moving. He'd know
he must strike this exact pose again and again.
She'd draw his face, full-lipped, lovely, strong chin blue
like Desperate Dan's, big eyes a child's not a man's,

would pay him a better rate than he is paying her
to sit unclothed looking at a cactus on his sill,
hands on her knees, feet planted at such an angle
he'll see her bleed, glancing up from his easel -

ruby lips parted, streak of ochre down his trouser leg,
one fist needled with little brushes, the other hand
darting - see the uncontrollable bead of
menses in the dark between her thighs.

Window-glass marble black. Night sky blocked out
by the room's reflection in which his head cocks
like a tom-tit as he measures an earlobe,
triangulates cheekbones, turns her soft face hard;

slow red tear dripping onto her chair-seat
as he screens himself off behind the canvas,
foot tapping to the climax of a sonata,
his elbows pointing out then disappearing.

Suki, Writer and Life Model

Hi Suki,

Jeremy who I was at St Martin's with gave me your number because I'm needing a model urgently for a series of Saturday life-drawing workshops in Harrogate. Our usual model's gone and broken her leg – it is in plaster! Could you give me a call back? It's Helen Peyton. £12 per hour and we can refund travel. Thanks! Bye now!

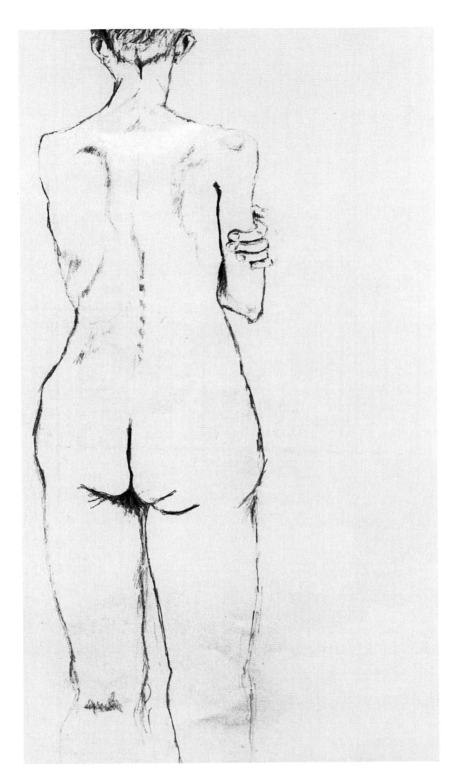

Melanie Alone - The Wait

I'm not keen on some of these big bottoms they're drawing.

My final bit of Arts Council grant is going on October's rent. Might get money for my beat-up Micra. Might not. My body's shaping up now I'm walking everywhere (since the tax disc ran out). I refuse Jeremy's cake these days.

I am dithering over whether to send Victoria a casual chatty email to see how she's getting on with *Melanie*.

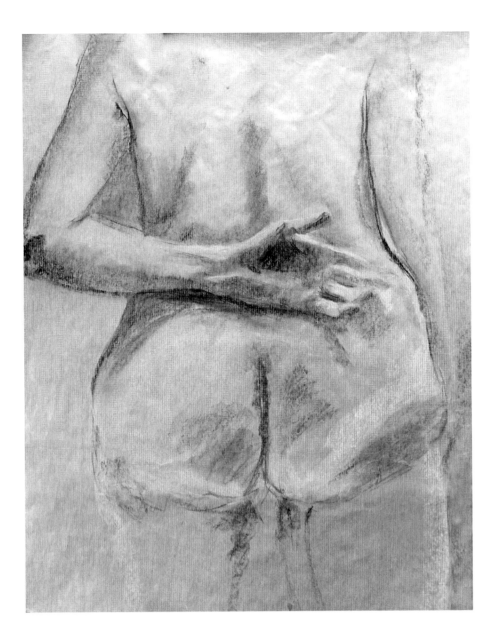

The worst thing that can happen

I think worse than starting to menstruate would be farting.

I'm not prone to fainting. And anyway fainting's not embarrassing.

I emailed Victoria and got an out-of-office reply – she'll be back a week on Monday.

Sex?

Sometimes when I am staring into space I am thinking about sex. I guess that's a taboo for a life model, but since I am not letting on to anyone about it I am not breaking the taboo. It cannot possibly be visible that I'm thinking about sex.

I say I'm thinking about my novel. Or a poem. Sometimes I am.

Do I check out the talent in the room? Yes.

Who wouldn't?

Melanie certainly would. My main character is unable to sustain a relationship and is sexually frustrated. I have her using a dildo and a vibrator simultaneously. I think I write erotica quite successfully.

I am still waiting to hear.

At Jeremy's

I don't follow the convention of using a dressing-gown. I use a long black tee-shirty frock. I would feel silly and also a bit provocative wearing something akin to bed-wear.

- Oh dash, I've forgotten my frock Jeremy. Sorry – I ran out of my house. Car's out of action. I need a bicycle.

Jeremy looks a bit horrified. I wonder why that is, Jeremy, you uptight person?

- A shirt'll do.

We both go to his bedroom ('changing room'). Jeremy reaches me a shirt off a hanger. I think it's his best shirt. A really nice shirt. He chucks it on the bed and races back to the warmed-up sitting room ('studio'). Jeremy's (rented) cottage is nearly as much of a hovel as my (rented) cottage.

At the end of the two hours I do something really stupid. I think it would be good to leave the scent of me on his shirt. I can only do this by rubbing the fabric of the shirt on me. Before I take it off I rub the under-arm seams into my armpits (which aren't sweaty, just Suki-smelling) then I pull the shirt over my head and get my bra and top clothing on at top speed (the 'dressing room' being perishing). I straighten out the shirt but, oh god, it's got whitish stains from my deodorant inside it at the armhole seams. I hadn't thought of that. I try to rub it off but it won't come off. It was a clean-washed shirt. Dark burgundy. The stains are really visible. He'll wonder how the hell I managed to sweat deodorant into it in the ten second descent from 'studio' to 'dressing room'.

Shipton College of Further Education

What ought a life model to say in an interview?

I hand over two print-outs of Jeremy's pictures of me and a drawing by one of the Harrogate punters that I snapped on my mobile. The Foundation Art and Design Course Team Leader looks at Jeremy's head and shoulders portrait and says 'early Stanley Spencer', and scrutinises his other, the second nude sketch. I brought the least fat one of the two.

Is Mr Team Leader staring at the drawing technique or at my body?

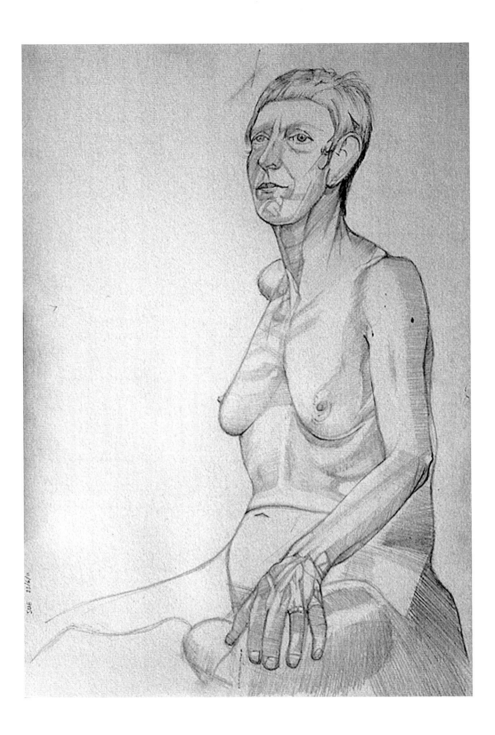

Leaving Jeremy's cottage, morning after Bonfire Night party

Yesterday Victoria emailed expressing enthusiasm and also reservations, and attached a document with a huge list of suggested amendments. I have to get my manuscript back to her when I have 'polished'.

Presumably she will sign me up if I do everything she suggests.

So I got drunk last night. Brilliant party.

Walking home through my glittering village on this frosty morning I feel so happy. Life modelling is the perfect way to support my writing life. My best day-job ever. Today I am going to immerse myself in my manuscript.

Getting fitter

The Micra has finally been towed away. The towing cost me thirty quid. I've blown December's rent on a second-hand folding bicycle. It is a beautiful and stylish item which will further enhance my fitness and will help me focus single-mindedly on transforming *Melanie Alone* into a perfect manuscript, and will altogether change my life for the better. I will no longer drink whisky alone; I will no longer need the pills.

Jeremy's network has thrown up more bookings, which makes up for the fact that I'm no longer modelling for him.

Kat My Very First Girlfriend's and Sybil her Civil Partner's opinions of Jeremy's pics which I have just emailed to them:

Suki! These are great. 'Finds me hideous'? I'm not so sure about that. I think he's captured a lot about you, which means he's seen it... Sybil likes the so-called 'fat' one best. She says 'tell Suki to put some weight back on' because you were looking a bit thin at our wedding. How's the novel coming? Got any more poems to send us? We love that.

Happy Christmas – you on your own? Best way. xxx

A solitary Christmas is actually what I need for getting the rest of Victoria's amendments done. Christmas Day will be just me and champagne and *Melanie Alone*. I'll have to pretend to the village that I've gone away though, or they'll all feel sorry for me.

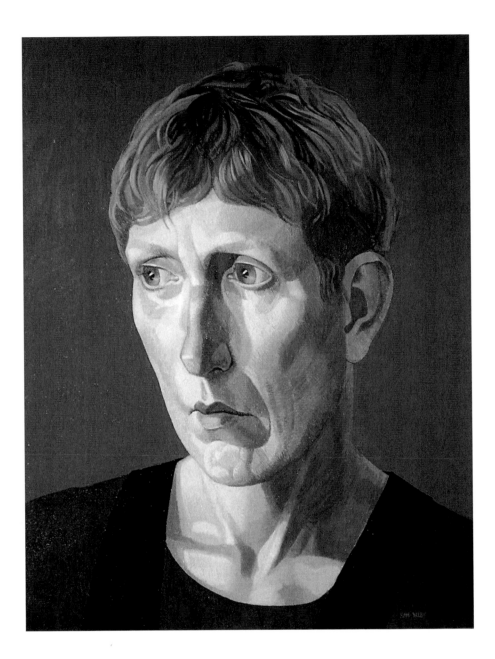

Winter

Suki the Rolling Stone

bijou studio apartment	old-fashioned grotty bedsit
central situation for easy commuting	seamiest corner of downtown Shipton
glass half full	glass half empty

The main thing is, it's the cheapest rental available on the planet.

On the plus side, living in Shipton I can bike it to most of my modelling bookings. Village life was a bit unstimulating anyway. The 'eviction' (that's what it felt like at least) and the trauma of the move and everything has pushed out my novel for a while. I need to get back into it.

Shipton College

Not warm, not well organised, not well paid. The Art Foundation class. I love it.

Shivery students keep leaving their easels to go warm their denimed bottoms on the long ineffectual radiators in this tin-roofed art room. They walk around my nakedness.

I am proud to be the most stoical life-model ever, nude amidst a throng of cosily muffled-up, snuffly students in fingerless gloves returning for further stints at their easels, bleating about the cold.

It is Tuesday. I now have both a morning and afternoon session. I sit in the canteen and instead of eating, work on my manuscript on my netbook. My plan is to get it back to Victoria before the Easter holiday. Her suggestions have stimulated me into a radical rewrite. This is good. I feel confident about the quality of my prose. It's becoming so much better.

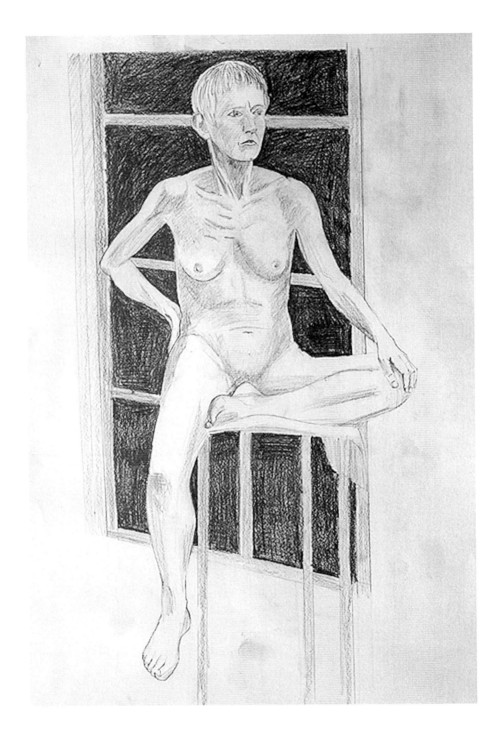

Beautiful

Even at break-time I get to write. I plug away at the odd poem on my netbook. A brief respite from *Melanie Alone*.

After the break, Team Leader Tristram dashes off a sketch to show the students how to do shading using a piece of charcoal sideways. I find it the most beautiful picture anyone has ever done of me. Maybe because it leaves my face off. I ask him if I can take a photo of it with my mobile.

Does the attractiveness of a portrait equate with the attraction felt by the artist for the model?

The drawing instructor's index finger

He uses it to draw her in the air,
warns of foreshortening, pointing at
the forward thrust of a knee, her twisting hips.
See the arc of the neck, the negative space
in her arm's crook, her weight
all on one foot, how her jaw nestles
into that left shoulder, these shadows
of ribs, the musculature, her bone structure

while she focuses on a rooftop
as they look hard, no shifting chairs, no sound,
him leaning nearer until her spiked-up hair
catches into his chin's bristle,
his finger – yellow, nicotined –
tracing a muscle a whisker from
her body's surface, the air moving,
her skin's pelt up on end.

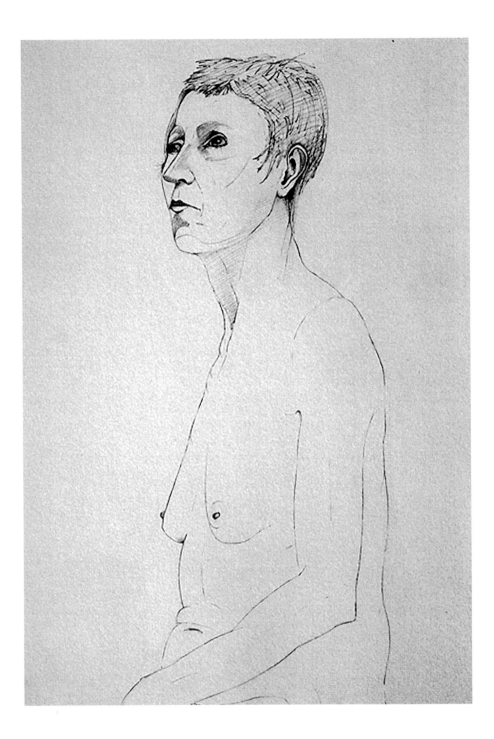

Foundation students

I am between poses, loitering at the centre of the circle of easels as everyone swaps over to new sheets of paper and passes round the masking tape, chatting.

Out of the blue Evelyn asks - so what made you and your girlfriend split up then?

Her voice is bell-like. Who can hear us? I stop myself from looking around. There is hubbub. Maybe nobody. I didn't realize I had divulged so much about myself. I have spoken more to Evelyn than other students, I suppose because she has spoken more to me. She's a bit more mature. And she does have the most gorgeous body in the room.

Autistic boys

Their easels are next to each other. They talk about their Aspergers while they are working. They are eighteen years old. One is very, very anal-retentive about drawing, taking too much time and care to get anything onto paper. The other (the beautiful one) not. In the end they both do lovely drawings. Gifted. I really like the one of my upper body and head. Ribby, with no eyes so that I look like a sculpture. The tutor manages to get Peter to give me it. At home I put it on the wall above my desk.

In *Melanie Alone*, Melanie gets off with a fifteen year-old boy with Aspergers Syndrome, one of her pupils. It's an illustration of her loneliness and her attraction to those whom she perceives to be as vulnerable as herself. It starts a chain of events that ends in her prosecution and attempted suicide.

In my earlier draft the boy spends a night in her bed and she only cuddles him, but she gets prosecuted for sex with a minor. In my rewrite however they do have sex. Victoria's suggestion.

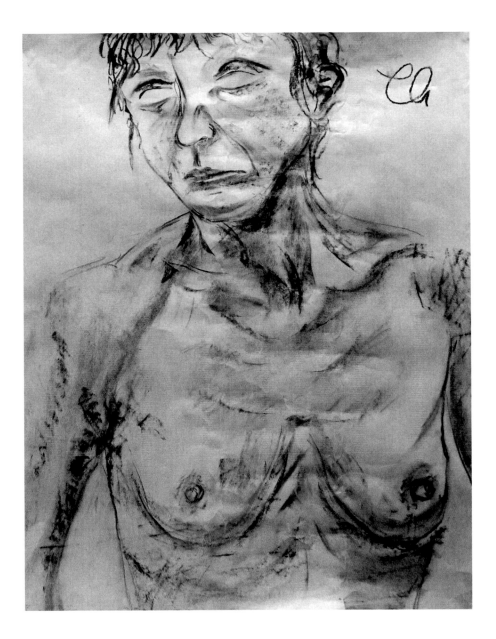

Breasts 1

The students are great at breasts. They are still being unlearned – trained in how not to draw what they have already preconceived, but what they can actually see. This morning – a straightforward seated pose – they give me the best breasts. Confidently drawing two big luscious circles without really looking at what's there.

Cycling home I drop in to Shipton Co-op (seller of the cheapest champagne in the land) and who should be at the check-out but autistic Peter, the floppy-forelocked one. I try to chat a bit. He is so endearingly awkward. I invite him for a coffee in Starbucks down the road but he gives me a perplexed look and stutters something unintelligible. Then he practically sprints out of the shop, leaving me feeling uneasy.

Breasts 2

In reality my breasts are starting to resemble the empty pockets of a starving Sudanese tribeswoman who has suckled fifteen children. They lie there with long creases down their sides where they meet the skin of my chest. Even the nipples sag in their wrinkly discs. Sometimes I induce a shiver in myself to make them hard. Perk them up for a while.

In bed at night, passing my hands over them, I can feel that they are not at all sexy. When I am laid on my back they are non-existent. I use my vibrator to make the nipples hard, imagining someone hanging over me, dragging his penis across them on its way to my mouth. But there is no actual breast – no flesh – for my ghost lover to get hold of.

I am fretful about the loss of them.

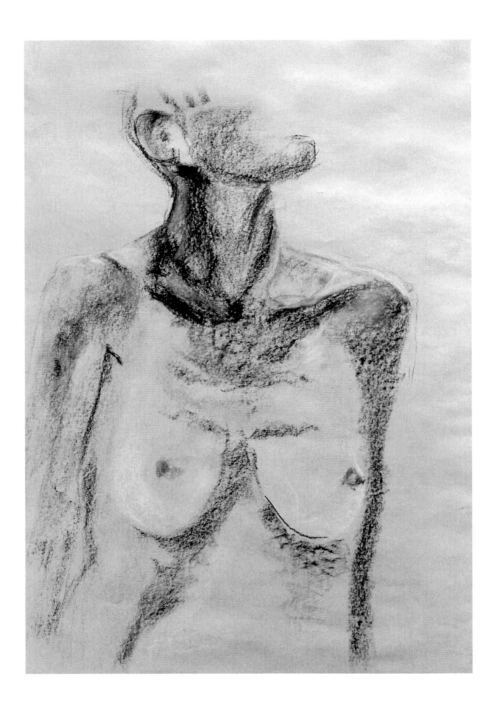

Filth

I am sitting on my toilet in the bedsit staring into the shower tray. Was it black like that when I moved in, or am I a slattern? Then I realise it is charcoal. The soles of my feet are thick with it.

I am hoping Victoria will approve of my having foregrounded Melanie's sexual fantasies and made them more explicit. One of her comments is that more sex would be good, because 'sexual odysseys' are currently in.

OFSTED

The college is on red alert.

Instead of taking my clothes off as usual in the middle of the art room I am using a 'changing cubicle' built in one corner out of a shifted bookcase, a giant-sized canvas and a bit of curtain. The art room is inhumanly tidy.

No-one can find the charcoal.

Peter's absence is commented on forlornly by his abandoned friend, and Tristram the tutor informs the whole class that Peter has changed his options and is doing printmaking instead. His eye momentarily meets mine.

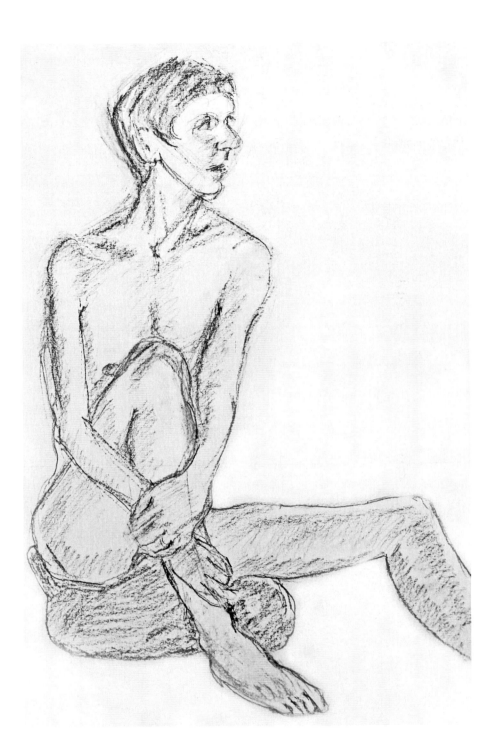

Post-OFSTED

The little blow-heater with the long snakey flex got hidden before the inspection, due to being a death-trap. They would have failed on Health and Safety.

But now it's lost.

And it's still February.

Warming myself

I have discovered that I can induce warmth from inside myself by dwelling on one of my Current Love Interests. Literally flush myself up and get warm.

Is it a woman warming me up or is it a man? I am indecisive. I want it all. My ghosts have their fingers or their members in me. I get my nipples teased into hardness by their tongues.

My nipple erection is visible to my audience. It will be put down to the cold. Or will my hard nipples arouse curiosity?

Or will they *arouse* anyone?

My Current Love Interests

To get warm, I work through them. Not my latest brief disaster – I blot that one out. So that leaves:

Current Love Interest No. 1 (Unrequited)

Current Love Interest No. 2 (easier to conjure, as we have had sex)

'Fabulous-Fling-That-Is-No-More'. Or maybe I should call that 'Most-Incredible-Night-Of-Sex-Of-My-Entire-Life'.

I re-live the latter in detail. I keep having to return to the moment to make sure I'm not moving in the manner required by my fantasy. No, I am still. So, back into her bed. No – onto my kitchen floor. Cold and hard like the one I'm standing on. I feel my face flush, and involuntary movement: my vagina clenching. I know my vagina isn't visible but my whole body is zinging. Maybe that's visible. Maybe there's something in my expression.

Being trapped in a pose is what makes my fantasy work. One or other of my lovers is touching me but I am not allowed to move. Even though I'm being entered. Fingers hooking into me as though into the small hard neck of a vase.

I go for heart-stopping cunnilingus with my beautiful girl while Current Love Interest No. 1 looks on. Until he too eventually comes up behind and enters me. I swap him then for Current Love Interest No. 2 who I think has a bigger penis.

It is cold, but this way I can bear the cold. Mental fucking in the cause of Art.

What drives men

I've just come away from my Kirkby Village Art Group booking with a fistful of notes, so I can replace my champagne. The fridge is empty without it.

Completely.

I finished off my previous bottle yesterday at Paolo and Nathan's. The celebration? My poem 'Artist drawing a pregnant woman' is Bridport shortlisted. Over eight thousand poems entered, less than two hundred on the shortlist. I do the maths (laboriously). I belong to the two-and-a-half per cent. Yey. I already knew that's where I belonged. The world needs to catch up with my knowledge.

The second stanza came out of Conservative Jeremy's mouth. God. What drives men.

Artist drawing a pregnant woman

Each sitting he sees a change in her stomach
and re-draws it, makes it exact, a perfect
object, the symmetry of its globe absolute,
its curve pure mathematics. He has charted
her collar-bones, delineated their shady pockets,
measured her chin and her nose's angle,
captured her forehead precisely.

Sometimes when stooping to pick up charcoal
or boiling the kettle, death comes out of nowhere,
grips him while he's holding a coffee cup
or right in the middle of cleaning brushes.
Death like a vice, arms pinned to sides,
muscles paralysed, breathing stopped, life
switched off, no spark left, his flat pitch-black.

How to control her, the way she spills over
on the chair's hard surface, that fractional swing
as she hangs like a pear on his paper,
filled-out skin shadowless, nipples gone soft,
each sitting worse: tonight she is nebulous,
bone-structure lost, all her hollows lost,
her belly rippling, dimpling.

Email bookings

Dear Suki, great session in Leeds! As said, would like to use your fantastic physique with my amateur group in Little Maltham Methodist Hall, any Thursday in March. We can pay £15 per hour. When are you free? Petronella x

I am rushing to complete my final draft and get it posted to Victoria's agency before Easter, as she'll probably be going away somewhere. So she'll be able to take it with her.

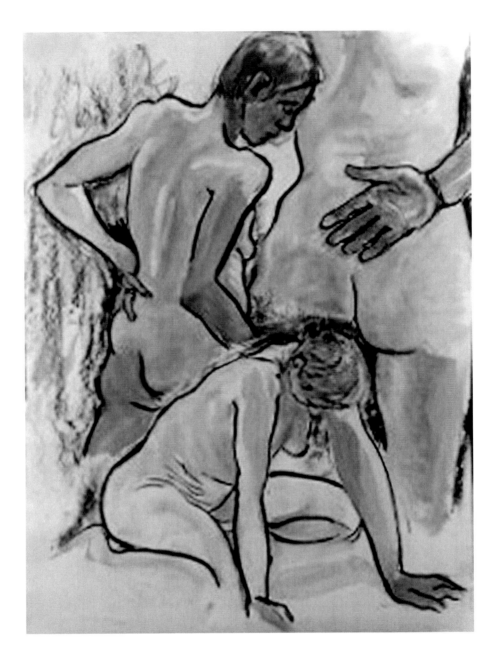

Current Love Interest No.1 (Unrequited)

I emailed him this pencil and watercolour sketch by one of the Leeds artists (and mentioned that I don't have any particular plans for Easter).

He emailed back – 'Fabulous. Strong. Thanks for sharing.'

So why doesn't he want me?

Belsen-esque

My ex-partner invents this word for my new physique – her take on it. We spend Easter together to avoid our families. Not good. She passes judgement on my Prozac. I pass judgement on her chain-smoking. I don't mention her exams. She doesn't mention my novel.

It's too soon. Not yet two years. Still too many issues.

In fact it's her fault I'm a scrawn-bag. She was my cook for seventeen years. She de-skilled me. I don't know how to feed myself.

Victoria emailed an acknowledgement of receipt!

Spring

Advice from a mature student in her fifties

I'm being your mother now. You've lost too much weight since last term. Hope you don't mind me saying so. Look after yourself.

She can't be my mother. She has no idea. I am forty blinking six.

I get home to find – huge excitement – an email from Victoria; the subject box says, 'By the way...'

I click on the message. She is advising me that I ought to prepare a one-page synopsis and that it needs to be perfect as it is the first (and sometimes only, if it doesn't impress) thing a publisher reads. I feel slightly deflated.

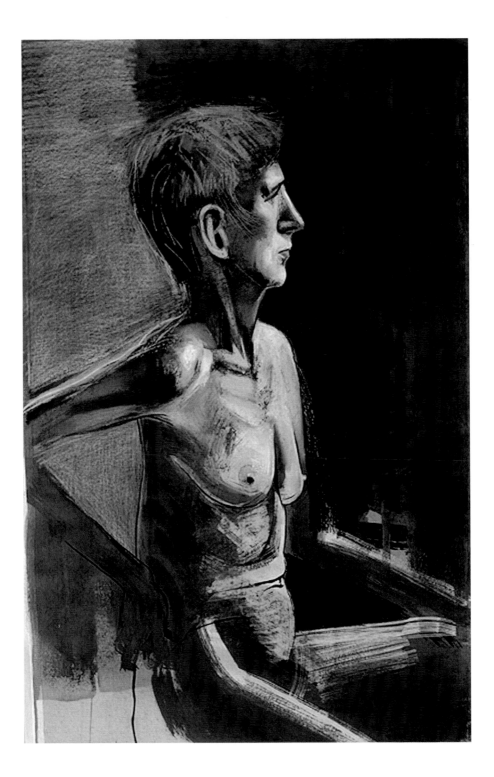

Shipton Castle

I cycle under the portcullis. The courtyard's shiny cobbles chuck me about. I fold up my bicycle and hoik it through the massive oak doors to be out of the April showers.

I expect it to be draughty but it's alright. Threadbare Persian carpet for the model to stand on. An unconventionally clean mattress for horizontal poses. The changing area is behind a moth-eaten tapestry slung across an alcove in which a cannon is being stored. Rough-hewn walls, flagstone floor, dusky light filtering in through the Perspex fixed over the arrow-slit. I drape my clothes on the cannon.

'Do small to big' says Sharon the tutor. I do the series of poses in which I unfold myself. Unfurl from foetal to a glorious tiptoe stretch.

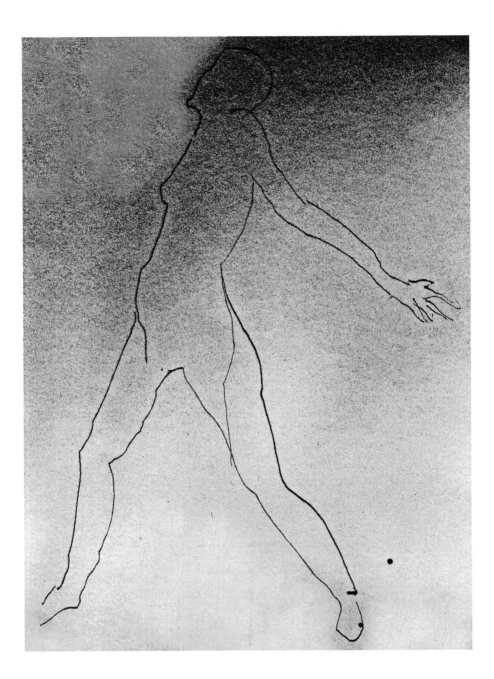

De-robing

Since ultra-formal Conservative Jeremy (who has moved on to a younger model), I avoid any sort of build-up to the De-Robing Moment. So prissy to clasp one's robe about oneself - or frock, in my case - until the very last second, after the pose has been decided on and 'practised'.

Writer's Bottom Rash 1

I have a run of late nights, perfecting my synopsis. At four in the afternoon the day before I do the Foundation class, I drag myself away from my PC and rush over to Boots.

-   I've got a red rash on my bottom and I'm life-modelling tomorrow morning. What can you give me to make it go away?

She consults with the chemist and comes back. They ought not to give me something, I should go see the nurse first.

-   Gosh, you must be very brave, she adds.

I race to the surgery on my bicycle. Amazingly I get to see the nurse within minutes.

-   Hmm. Doctor needs to check this. It's late opening tonight, go to the desk and ask to see someone.

I get an appointment. I come back to the surgery at seven in the evening. I flip up my skirts, pull my knickers down. My rash flashes red in his face. It turns out that sitting at my PC for far too many hours in recent weeks has created a sweaty micro-climate between my skin and the spongy seat of my desk stool, enabling bacteria to thrive in the hair follicles of my bottom.

I am prescribed antibiotics. It will not be gone by morning.

Writer's Bottom Rash 2

I pull off my tee-shirt dress and stand in the centre of the room with my hands covering my buttocks, trying to look natural.

First pose: crouched. Bottom tucked under. Maybe only one or two of the further-flung lumpy blotches visible.

Second pose: standing, hands on buttocks.

Third pose: standing with a different twist to my torso, hands on buttocks.

When the end of the pose is called – *thank you Suki. Back here in fifteen minutes please, folks* – I catch the eye of the nice woman who is fifty-something, the mature student, and grin.

-    I've got this rash on my bum.

-    I know.

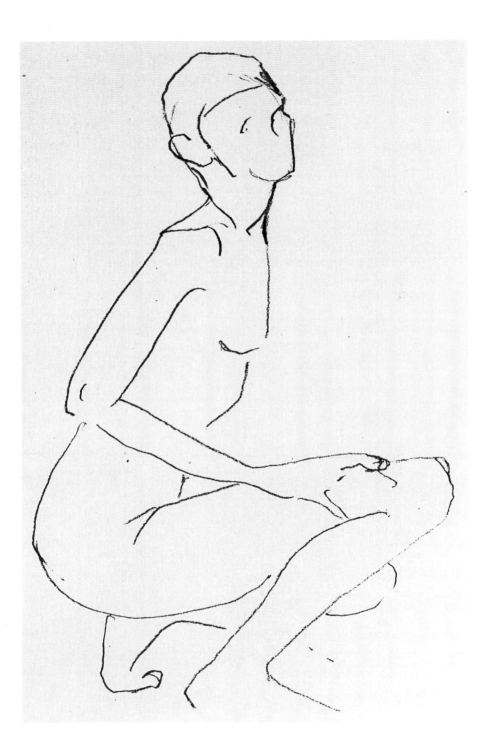

Seventy-five minutes

This is the longest pose I have ever done. They are greedy. The Professionals. They've got studios in remote Dales barns. They live by their art.

I like how they are so engrossed in me. They are single-minded. They are the only group who don't make themselves drinks halfway through. Because they are focused. Driven. This is their real life. Their drawings are awesome.

I will not say. I *will not say* how much this hurts.

I ask around the group for anyone who'd like to do a 'skills exchange' instead of money: I can offer some hours of modelling in return for anyone who will come and build me a bookcase. This guy Steve who shares a studio with his wife, a weaver, jumps at it.

Narcissistic? *Moi?*

I, too, am greedy. I want all these pictures. I've been snapping them on my mobile phone. The quality's not great but I print them out anyway and Blutack them round my desk.

Sometimes I ask permission. Sometimes I do it surreptitiously because I am embarrassed to ask. What will they think?

The synopsis: as advised, and with great difficulty, I have kept it to a mere one side of A4. It is as perfect as I can get it. I email it as an attachment, and get an immediate acknowledgement of receipt from Lara, Administrative Assistant.

Relaxed

I've got into this really comfortable position on all fours, like a happy dog. I could stay like this for ages.

After a while I start thinking about my anus. That it's probably visible. My buttocks are a bit spread in this position, and are nowadays reduced in flesh; not the big flubbery cheeks they used to be.

I don't know who's behind me. Somebody is. Are they standing at their easel or seated? What angle are they at? What can they see? Might they catch sight of my messy anus? Someone is probably going – oh my god, what is that.

I think of it as a spent tulip – one which has fully opened and then gone over-ripe and petalled out wantonly. Nothing neat and pert about it any more. A very red tulip. A petaline abundance. A doctor told me that there is one haemorrhoid while the rest of the mess of flappy layers is skin tags.

Anyone who likes a girl to be in doggie position would have to find this tulip configuration – well, at least not off-putting.

Maybe someone will highlight it, colour it scarlet.

Am I embarrassed?

No. I'm feeling good about myself; in fact about life, the universe, everything.

Behind the curtain…

…the toilet.

When I arrive at Steve's studio I pull my folding bicycle through the front door of the shop (it's a shop. The main street is a flimsy bit of white sheet away) and ask for the loo. This is the first of two one-to-one sessions to pay him back in kind for building my bookcases. His wife Emma is trundling away on her loom upstairs. Woman's Hour is on somewhere. Steve's got the pot-bellied stove going.

-   Here it is.

The toilet. In the room. Behind a piece of cloth. Would I like a cup of tea?

I amaze myself. I unclench no trouble at all. Steve turns out to be the type of person I can wee almost-in-front of.

That says a lot.

'The Man in the Blue Scarf'

Steve lends me this book everyone's reading. It's by art critic Martin Gayford, about his relationship to Lucien Freud during the period when he was sitting for a portrait.

Me and Steve have a good conversation about The Man in the Blue Scarf. We talk about the dynamic between artist and model, as Steve potters away at the canvas, our conversation interspersed with Steve's sharp little looks, sighs and mutterings, the odd oath. We talk like pals in the pub. It stays abstract. Not about us, our dynamic. We agree the artist-model relationship is a sensual one. How could it not be. Martin Gayford was clothed, yet his account describes an intimacy that is quasi-physical – 'the little mapping movements of [Freud's] brush tingle on my face, deliberative'.

Steve covers the historical ground. The tradition of artists and models having sexual relationships. The question of who seduces whom. Emma is trundling away upstairs, we will all eat lunch together shortly. The tone is matey, comfortable. Steve expresses his opinions in an almost derangedly emphatic way. I like him.

How common is it, this thing of artists having sex with their models?

Twosome

The one-day workshop has accidentally double-booked me with a woman called Marilyn. The decision is to pay both of us and have us pose together.

Marilyn has a mass of long blond curls. She has buoyant pointy breasts like lemons. She has a rose tattoo down her back. Her pubic hair is waxed into a neat shape. When we get undressed, she puts on a mini-kimono and sequinned slippers. She is dainty.

Her skin is pink, mine is blue. She is the girl, I am the boy.

In my novel there is a scene in which Melanie self-harms after a female colleague rejects her advances.

Butch-femme

We stand on the podium not exactly back to back. I am tall, skinny, angular. She is smaller, softer. From my left shoulder to the floor, my side is touching her side. Her hair is whisping against my back. Our skins hover against each other, trembly, lightly touching then parting then touching. We are not at all still. I wonder whether the punters can see it. The dynamic.

At the end of the session Marilyn offers to email me details of other places I can get work. We exchange addresses, pulling on clothes behind the screen while also fumbling about for pens and bits of paper. I unbalance and knock into her. I catch her eye for longer than is necessary. She looks at me as though I've got two heads. There is real fear.

My bedsit has a whiff of decaying human. I think it's my unwashed, dampish bedding. I have yet to open a window. Spring has been freezing.

With the synopsis now out of the house, the un-slept-in side of my double bed is covered with notes for poems, A4 sheets that shift and and slide to the floor when I turn over in the night.

Subject

Hold out your pencil and look at me,
measure angles, how my thigh hangs,
white shins, rib-bones, nipples,
rippled stomach, this patch of scrappy hair,
but do not adjust my pose using your hands
or ask after my other life, or offer your
home-made flapjack, nor expect me to like
your artwork, nor to smile at you
or blush instead of looking straight back.

You fetch a palette thick with paint and
knife it on, eyes flicking up from the canvas,
eyes that clunk and lock with mine like
machine parts then disengage
as you score into it.

Desperate Dan

Regarding the tradition of artists seducing their models, or models seducing the artists – whichever it is.

It happened.

With Conservative Jeremy. Gifted Jeremy of the Pent-Up Passion. Muscular, athletic, young, macho Jeremy-Of-Few-Words.

It was whisky. It was the Bonfire Party. He was up for it. A night on the hearthrug in front of his coal burner. He was sick halfway through.

Stupidly though, I got attached, due to that girl thing of thinking sex is meaningful. And he hated me for that, so didn't employ me again.

In the morning when we woke up he pulled me back on top of him. He definitely did want me.

Summer

Moments of happiness

Last summer I had a size 14 bottom. Now I'm an 8. I hear such wonderful adjectives: elegant, graceful, slender, willowy, lovely. Swan-like neck. Leggy. Toned. Muscular.

'*Gorgeous* pose.'

'Are you a dancer?'

The Real Truth

A cleaner is talking to another cleaner, waving at the sketches on the art room wall, when I walk in.

\-   Scrawny, isn't she.

One negative word has the power of ten positive ones.

I sent the synopsis to Victoria nearly seven weeks ago. Her lack of communication is making me anxious.

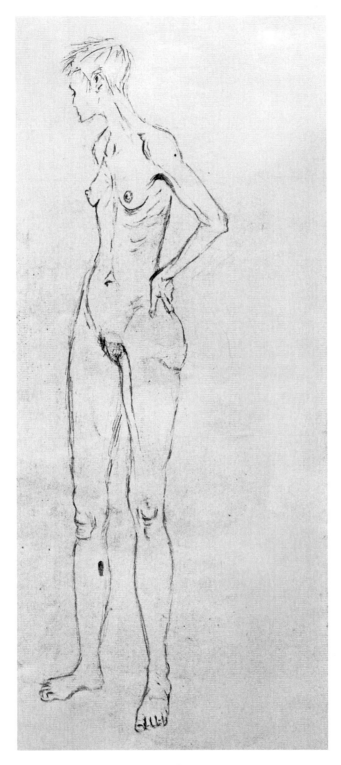

101

I do have friends 1

Penelope, a textile artist back in my village, wants to sew me. After a strenuous ninety minutes my three-gear folding bicycle gets me to her barn conversion on the windswept moor top. A tree-less, granite-ridden landscape. Under this miserable late-June sky, all is greyscale, bleak, watery.

A great setting for contemplating my novel's main theme.

She offers lunch. I say I don't eat cheese. She offers bread. I say I've already had my carbs today (porridge oats mixed with my breakfast banana and soya milk). As an afterthought I add I've eaten lunch anyway. She asks after the novel. I say it's now back with this high-powered agent for whom I did a radical rewrite and that I'm just waiting to hear.

-    Fingers crossed! says Penelope.

When I am in pose I can see the roof of Conservative Jeremy's cottage down by the river.

-    That was a deep sigh, Suki!

The image Penelope makes of me is a kind one.

I do have friends 2

Before cycling back to Shipton I have a latte in Paolo and Nathan's sumptuous manor.

- We just hope you're not getting into any unhealthy patterns, Suki, that's all, says Paolo.

- I'm fine. Look, watch this!

I eat a truffle.

- We hope you don't mind us saying this? You don't want to make yourself ill. You're beautiful.

- Oh, so are you two!

I kiss them both.

Threshington Memorial Hall

For some it is their first time. When I pull off my black tee-shirt dress, startlingly somebody whoops. Ruby the tutor advises the group – don't be put off by the fact that she's got no clothes on. Just think of her as a table.

Thirty minutes in, two ladies leave their drawings to go make the tea. At break-time I am handed my own plate of five chocolate biscuits.

I eat three, then feel horribly anxious. If I were bulimic I would throw them up. But I'm not.

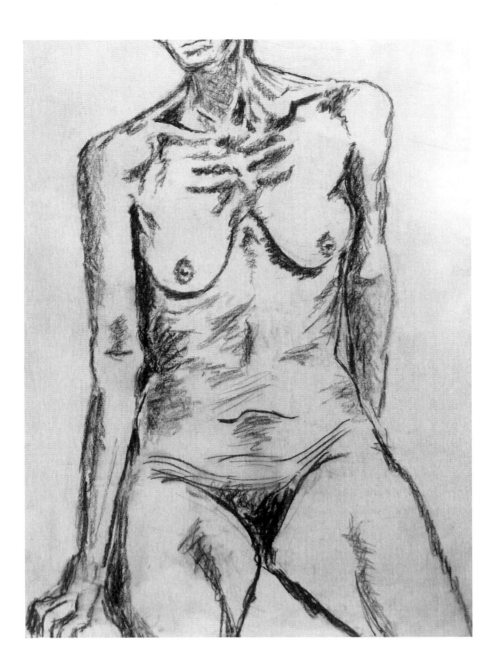

Fragile

I look like an emaciated child.

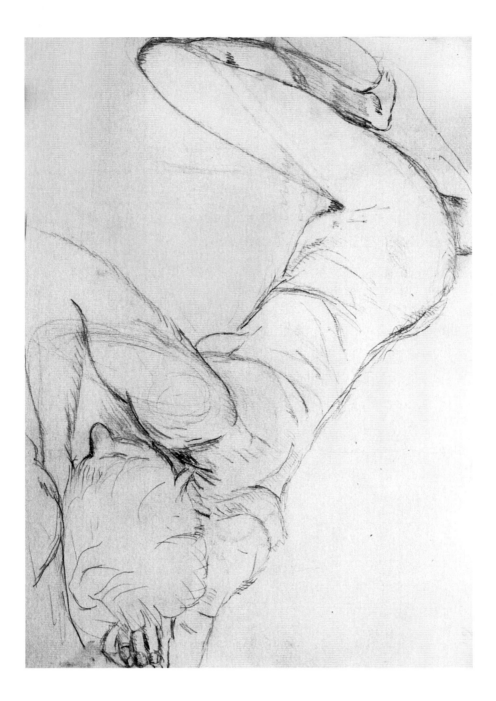

Over-written

This is Victoria's verdict. By email. She gives a long list of reasons and excuses for being unable, after much heart-searching, to sign me up. In the current climate. In this time when it is so difficult to place even the latest novels of her well-established clients.

I'm dwelling on all this while in-pose and it's bloody hot. There's no fan. The punters will be watching the liquid I feel trickling out of my pubic hair and down my inner thighs and they will be thinking that it is wee, not perspiration.

Am I embarrassed?

No.

Why not?

Because we're all just bloody animals. Fuck it.

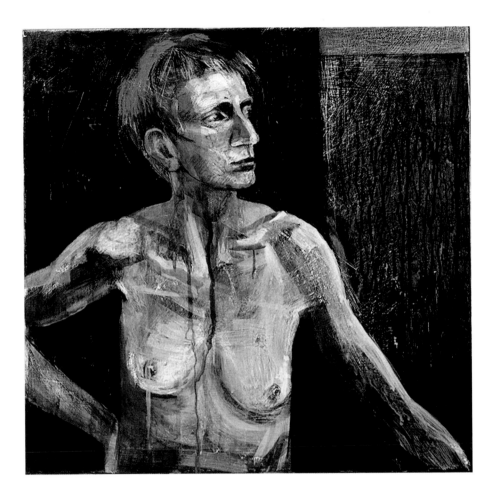

Ugly

I look like a monkey.

When I get home my manuscript is there on the mat. Like a dead body.

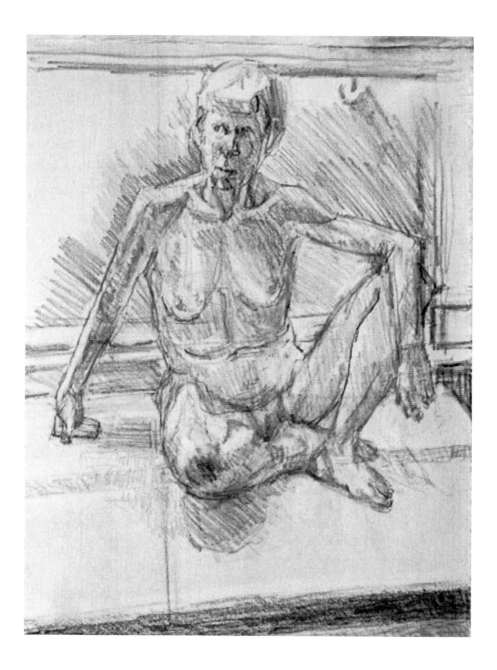

The faint

Ten easels in a circle,
flex snaking to the centre, fan-heater's
tilted-up cobra-head, its hot jet
on her chicken legs, her bloated feeling
from not eating. She shivers

as they try out charcoal on her,
on big cheap paper, blacking in fishy ribs,
puckered-up nipples, empty skin rippling,
her breasts little pockets, pelvis jutted out,
neck swanlike, eyes whippetish,

each week better and better at measuring,
really getting her – one bold stroke a leg,
her arching back, neck stretched giraffesque
or like an elephant's trunk held erect,
its thin skin ever more taut

until she crumples onto the floorboards –
abstract smatterings round her head like stars,
thick smear of ochre under her — the day she drops
flat out on a Pollock, no-one able to save her,
not all the talent in that room.

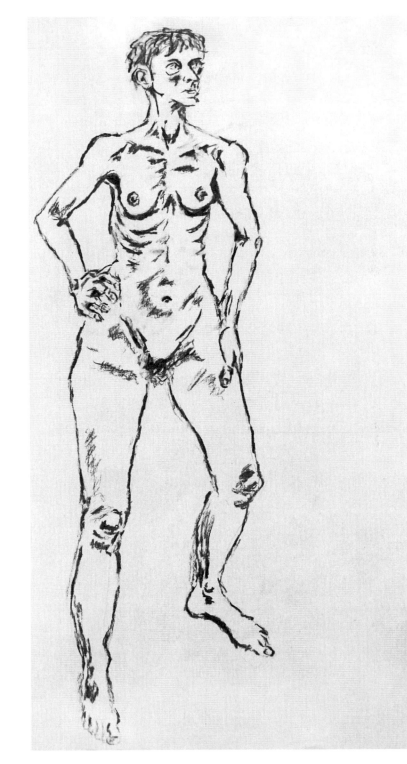

Black

I go to the bus station and find out the cheapest journey to any seaside place. And so arrive in Filey.

In the rain.

This is not exactly a B&B, not exactly a hostel. There's a chilly shared kitchenette at the end of a poky corridor. It has a microwave, a kettle and a Baby Belling stove. It is desolately clean. The bedroom has a single bed with a slippy nylon quilt (purple), a crappy old wardrobe with a door that swings open, a modern cheap washbasin in a shell-shape, a miniscule soap-bar in waxed paper. The view is of a back yard with wheely bins and another guest-house's back yard with wheely bins and a sliver of grey sea visible over the roof. The divisions of rooms into smaller rooms using cheap partitioning means the house is claustrophobic, and it is smelly. Sweet, synthetic smells: fabric conditioner, air freshener, toilet deodorant. Like childhood.

And over the bed is one of those Monet nudes. A fat woman, whale-like, greenish-hued, on a watery background.

I've brought hardly anything: my folding bicycle and my netbook and dongle – those three things just out of habit. And two pairs of knickers (I've told the owner two days but have only paid for the first night). And my three-quarters of a bottle of whisky and three blister packs of aspirin, about fifty tablets.

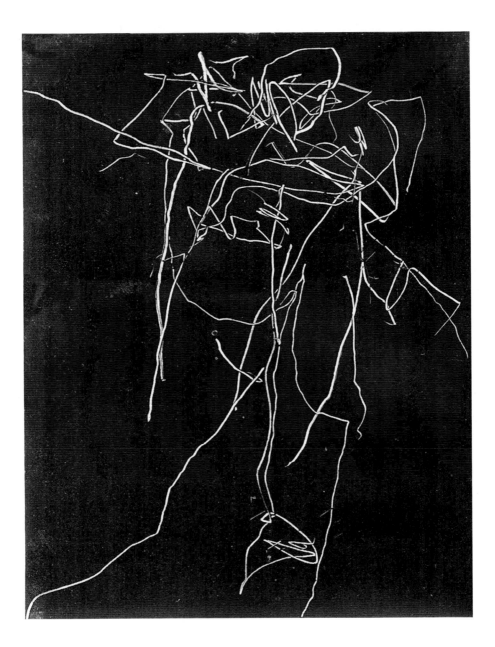

Blacker

I think about being a loser.

I get under the slippy quilt with my clothes and shoes on.

I go over everybody. (Not-So-) Current Love Interest No. 1 who finds me physically grotesque. Current Love Interest No. 2 who has gone to live in another country, and anyway is too... Conservative Jeremy who hates me. Best Sex Ever Girl who hasn't responded to emails for at least eighteen months.

I didn't bring my vibrator. I finger myself but am too miserable to get into it.

I think about my novel. It's crap. And there's no point. Even if it gets published, what does it do? Who does it touch? What is it for? What is this life? What the fuck am I doing? Why?

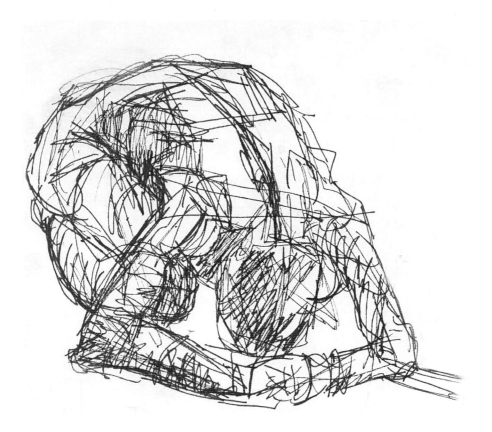

Back on the bus

I did this same thing one year ago in Morecambe.

I feel really really bad. Alcohol poisoning.

Morning after 47th birthday

The thing is, today is brilliant sunshine.

It is shining into the bus.

Almost home

I will curl up in my armchair. I will drink tea in it and read some poetry. Then I'll post out my chapters to another agent.

As I bang in, my bike wheel picks up a piece of paper on the mat.

Emma has left me. Came for tea and sympathy.

Steve

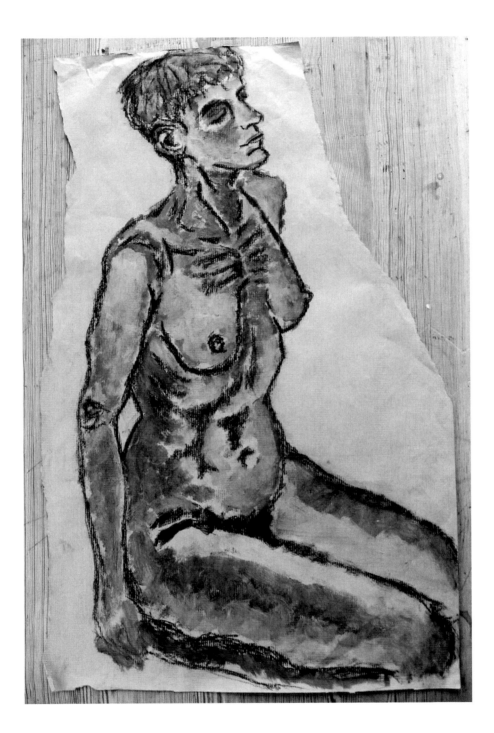

Contributing Artists

Hadyn Bradbury attends life-drawing classes at Redbrick Mill. Hadyn's work can be viewed at tomwood.typepad.com.

Carine Brosse is a full-time artist living in Grassington. Inspired by the darker fairy-tales. Influences include Bourgeois, Rego, Rauschenberg, Giacometti, Messager, Svankmajer, the Quay Brothers and early Polanski films. See onceuponatimeetc.com

David Cook paints, prints, lives and works in the Yorkshire Dales. He draws with the Grassington Group who meet at Threshfield. Residency at Jyvaskyla Print Centre Finland 2011. A.R.C.A. see www.artdc.co.uk

Sandra Cowper BA (Hons) studied Art as a mature student at Wakefield College and Bretton College, combining her love of painting and sculpture. Now retired she has more freedom to concentrate on life drawing and painting See www.tomwood.typepad.com

Sam Dalby graduated from Cleveland College of Art and Design (1997) and is a reputed as a portrait painter. Exhibitions include BP Portrait Award (2003), Royal Society of Portrait Painters (2010, 2011). Sam offers tutoring in portraiture. www.samdalby.co.uk

Eliza Dear waited till her seventies to become the artist she wanted to be. At present her work is exploring bold colour and patterns.

Val Emmerson SRN, SCM, BA (Hons) painted throughout her twenty years as a general nurse and midwife before obtaining a degree in Textile Design. Val now paints and runs a busy B&B business, and has exhibited widely.

Lisa Etherington attended Bournemouth Art School in the mid 'sixties, then learned print making in Bradford. Exhibitions include Bradford Open. She is a long-standing member of the Saturday People life-drawing group, Leeds. Art for Lisa is a therapeutic hobby, and life-drawing a worthwhile discipline. See saturdaypeople.org.uk

Cathy Everett attends life-drawing classes at Redbrick Mill. Cathy's work can be viewed at tomwood.typepad.com.

Jane Fielder is an artist and runs The Bingley Gallery thebingleygallery.com. She has organised a life-drawing group for many years.

Susan Forster Ross studied in Liverpool, Chelsea, Leeds. Loves Art, people, landscape, colour, sequins, glitter and teaches drawing, painting, life drawing and fitness in West Yorkshire, inspired by the human face and form. See saturdaypeople.org.uk.

Phil Fraser attends the Grassington Group.

Edie Gardner completed an Art Foundation year and now writes stories and poems, explores the world of dreams, does yoga, and sings *chansons* to herself and anyone who will listen. She is studying reflexology and holistic therapy. Edie has a room by the sea and still does life-drawing.

Ivan Goldsmith is an international Design Consultant and Design Director of Artic Storm Ltd, Art Consultants specialising in the hotel, leisure and commercial sectors. He attends life-drawing classes at Redbrick Mill. See his work at tomwood.typepad.com

Tom Graham produced his contribution to this book at the age of seventeen and attended an Art Foundation course at Craven College, Skipton, in 2012.

Danny Handzij completed his Foundation year at Craven College in 2011.

Lavinia Hardy works in many media, including painting, ceramics, paper and textiles. Her inspiration has been our interconnection with the natural world, and its Creator, reflected in both symbolic and landscape images. Lavinia attends the Grassington Group.

Christine Holgate began painting in Hong Kong in the 1960s. Since returning to England she has enjoyed the company and stimulation of Yorkshire artists, and has branched out into portraiture. Christine attends the Grassington Group.

Kate Holland gained her BA (Hons) in Fine Art and retired after many years of teaching at adult, then secondary, levels (Art, Information Technology). Kate completed a HNC Textile course at Craven College, and was part of the Little Green Textiles exhibition at the Gallery on the Green, Settle. galleryonthegreen.org.uk

Nick Holmes, a retired accountant, exchanged the struggle to balance the figures in his professional life with the rather more artistic challenge of capturing figures in a number of life-drawing classes in and around Bradford.

Sue Ibbotson attends life-drawing classes at Redbrick Mill because 'it is a relaxing pass-time and a great bunch of people'. Sue's work can be viewed at tomwood.typepad.com.

Ralph Linney attends the Cullingworth life drawing group.

Keith Lowe specialises in portrait and figurative work using water-based media, pastels and oils. He is a member of the Saturday People, Leeds. Work can be viewed at saturdaypeople.org.uk and keithlowe.co.uk

Russell Lumb, retired architect, has been life-drawing for forty years. He is now working with acrylic and oils to make life paintings and abstract landscape. He is a member of the Redbrick Mill Life Group. Russell's work can be viewed at tomwood.typepad.com.

Chris Murray trained in Visual Communication, Bath Academy of Art. Lives in Skipton. Member, Brighton Independent Printmakers. Has exhibited at the Castor & Pollux Gallery, Harewood House, Leeds Open, Harvey Nichols (Leeds), and 'Muse' (Brighton Festival Fringe) etc. See brightonbreezy.co.uk/chrismurray.html

Tony Noble is a full-time artist. Exhibitions: BP Portrait Award 2008, 2010, 2011; Royal Society of Portrait Painters 2010, 2011; ING Discerning Eye 2010, 2011; *Sunday Times* Watercolour Competition 2009, 2010; Ruth Borchard Self-Portrait Exhibition 2011. Tony's studio is at Redbrick Mill where for his sins he organizes the models for the life drawing group. www.tonynoble-artist.com

Judi Rich completed a Foundation course in Art & Design at Craven College specialising in Fine Art (2008) and continues to develop her work through life-drawing and portraiture classes around Otley and Ilkley and through the tutelage of Jane Parkin SWA, SEqA. Portraiture is a passion, looking to capture 'the essence'.

Kate Stewart works in watercolour and textiles. For Kate, life drawing is a delight, an impossible task and an essential basic skill. katestewart-art.blogspot.com

Justyn Tandy BA (Hons), Fine Art, Loughborough College of Art and Design; MA, History of Art, Warwick University. Currently Team Leader, Foundation Studies course in Art and Design and HND course in Fine Art, Craven College, Skipton. Specialisms: Drawing, Painting, and History of Art and Design. Current research interests encompass ideas of depiction and perception in Art.

David Thomas, born in West London; trained in Cheltenham, Cardiff and Leeds; has lived in Wales, Worcestershire, Gloucestershire, Kenya, Cornwall and Devon. David has painted since 1984 and uses still-life as a way of exploring and understanding the nature of visual perception. See junctionworkshop.co.uk

Joanna Thompson lives and works in Skipton, North Yorkshire. She was born in Ashby-de-la-Zouch and studied Fine Art at Leeds Metropolitan University. Joanna is a painter whose interest lies in the still life genre. She attends the Grassington Group.

Shirley Y. Warrenberg trained in Book Illustration at Leeds College of Art and taught in London, then the north. Now retired, Shirley works in a variety of media. Subjects include the Yorkshire Dales, floral studies, life-drawings and portraits. A member of Cullingworth Art Club, Shirley has also exhibited with Ilkley Art Club.

Helen Wheatley produces watercolours and drawings of architecture and traditional sailing ships, exploring the interplay between formal structure and transient atmospheric effects. She has been a set designer, art teacher, sailor and theatre stage manager as well as a painter. Helen attends the Grassington Group. See helenwheatley.co.uk

Paul Whitaker finds life drawing fascinating as an attempt to capture the essence of a person in just a few marks on paper. He attends the Cullingworth Group. See https:// sites.google.com/site/paulsgallery987654/

Tom Wood trained at Sheffield School of Art. Co-founder, Northern Academy of Art based at Redbrick Mill. Exhibits worldwide. National Portrait Gallery commissions for portraits of Professor Lord Robert Winston, Alan Bennett. Featured artist, BBC 'Star Portraits' arts programme painting actress Barbara Windsor. tomwood-art.com, tomwood.typepad.com

Alison Woods spent her first life as a scientist. She now paints and draws for pleasure in the Yorkshire Dales. Capturing the essence of our wild scenery is her main preoccupation, but figure work has enduring appeal and fascination. She attends the Grassington Group.